This book belongs to

From episodes of the animated TV series *Franklin*, produced by Nelvana Limited, Neurones France s.a.r.l. and Neurones Luxembourg S.A., based on the Franklin books by Paulette Bourgeois and Brenda Clark.

Franklin is a trademark of Kids Can Press Ltd.
The character Franklin was created by Paulette Bourgeois and Brenda Clark.

The Franklin Annual: Volume 1
© 2002 Context*x* Inc. and Brenda Clark Illustrator Inc.

This book includes the following stories first published in 2000:
Franklin's Bicycle Helmet
Franklin Forgets
Franklin Helps Out
Franklin and the Hero

All text © 2000 Context*x* Inc.
All illustrations © 2000 Brenda Clark Illustrator Inc.

Franklin's Bicycle Helmet TV tie-in adaptation written by Eva Moore. Illustrated by Sean Jeffrey, Mark Koren, Alice Sinkner and Jelena Sisic. Based on the TV episode *Franklin's Bicycle Helmet*, written by Nicola Barton.

Franklin Forgets TV tie-in adaptation written by Sharon Jennings. Illustrated by Sean Jeffrey, Mark Koren, Alice Sinkner and Jelena Sisic. Based on the TV episode *Franklin Takes the Blame*, written by Nicola Barton.

Franklin Helps Out TV tie-in adaptation written by Paulette Bourgeois. Illustrated by Sean Jeffrey, Mark Koren and Jelena Sisic. Based on the TV episode *Franklin's Nature Hike*, written by Nicola Barton.

Franklin and the Hero TV tie-in adaptation written by Sharon Jennings. Illustrated by Sean Jeffrey, Mark Koren, Jelena Sisic and Shelley Southern. Based on the TV episode *Franklin and the Hero*, written by Shane MacDougall.

All rights reserved. No part of this publication may be reproduced, stored in a retrieval system or transmitted, in any form or by any means, without the prior written permission of Kids Can Press Ltd. or, in case of photocopying or other reprographic copying, a license from CANCOPY (Canadian Copyright Licensing Agency), 1 Yonge Street, Suite 1900, Toronto, ON, M5E 1E5.

Kids Can Press acknowledges the financial support of the Ontario Arts Council, the Canada Council for the Arts and the Government of Canada, through the BPIDP, for our publishing activity.

Kids Can Press Ltd..
29 Birch Avenue
Toronto, ON M4V 1E2

www.kidscanpress.com

Edited by Tara Walker and David MacDonald
Designed by Stacie Bowes

Printed in Hong Kong, China, by Wing King Tong Company Limited

CDN 02 0 9 8 7 6 5 4 3 2 1

ISBN 1-55337-530-0

Kids Can Press is a **Corus**™ Entertainment company

The Franklin Annual

Kids Can Press

Contents

Franklin's Bicycle Helmet

FRANKLIN could count by twos and tie his shoes. He could zip zippers and buckle buckles. But Franklin couldn't buckle up his bicycle helmet anymore. It was too small.

Franklin's mother took him to the store to get a new helmet. There were rows and rows of helmets to choose from. Franklin picked a silver and white one with a flashing red light on top.

"This is the one I want!" he said.

Franklin's mother checked the fit. It was just right.

"Are you sure you like this helmet?" she asked. "It's a little flashy."

"I think it's great," Franklin replied.

"Okay," said his mother. "If that's the one you want, that's the one we'll get."

Franklin did a happy dance.

That afternoon, Franklin practised his hand signals for the Bike Safety Rally.

"You're going to do fine tomorrow," said Franklin's father. "And I think Constable Raccoon will be impressed with your new helmet."

Franklin smiled proudly. "I can't wait to show it to my friends," he said.

The next morning, Franklin took his time getting to the rally. He wanted all his friends to be there when he arrived. He planned to surprise everyone with his new helmet.

When he got to the schoolyard, Franklin hid behind some bushes. He could hear his friends talking.

"Have you seen those funny helmets with the flashing light on top?" asked Fox.

"I wouldn't wear one," said Beaver. "You'd look like a fire engine with one of those on your head."

Suddenly, Franklin wasn't so sure about his new helmet. He took it off and hung it on his handlebar.

Franklin left his bicycle behind the bushes and walked over to his friends.

"Where's your bike?" asked Beaver.

"Um, I got a flat tire," Franklin fibbed. "I can't ride in the rally," he added sadly.

"You can borrow my bike," offered Bear. "My helmet, too."

Franklin cheered up. "Okay, Bear!" he said. "Thanks!"

Constable Raccoon blew his whistle. It was time for the rally to begin. The riders pushed their bikes toward the starting gate.

"What's that noise?" asked Fox.

"That's my bike," Rabbit said proudly. "I put cardboard in the wheel. Now my bike sounds like a motorcycle."

"Or like a piece of cardboard is stuck in your wheel," said Fox. He and Beaver laughed and ran ahead.

Rabbit looked embarrassed. "Maybe I should take the cardboard out," he said.

"I think it sounds neat," said Franklin.

"You do?" asked Rabbit. "I like it, too."

Rabbit thought for a moment, then made up his mind. "My bike is going to stay just the way it is!" he declared.

Constable Raccoon went over the safety rules. "And anyone who finishes the course without making a mistake will earn a shiny safety sticker," he announced.

Everyone was excited.

Fox was the first to get a sticker. Then Beaver and Rabbit earned their prizes. Bear did a perfect job, too.

14

Finally, it was Franklin's turn. He stepped forward with Bear's bike and helmet.

"Hold on, Franklin," said Constable Raccoon. "That helmet is too big for you. A helmet should fit snugly to give proper protection."

Franklin was disappointed.

"I'm sorry, Franklin," said Constable Raccoon, "but it wouldn't be safe for you to ride with that helmet. There will be another rally soon. I'll keep this sticker for you until then. Okay?"

Franklin nodded sadly. The rally was over.

Franklin was helping Constable Raccoon pack up when he noticed Rabbit behind the bushes. Rabbit had found his helmet!

Franklin raced over. "What are you doing?" he cried, snatching the helmet away.

Rabbit was surprised. "Is that yours?" he asked.

"Yes," Franklin admitted, "but I don't want anyone making fun of it."

"I won't make fun of it," said Rabbit. "I think it's amazing."

"You do?" said Franklin. He sighed. "So do I."

Franklin looked at his helmet for a minute. Then he put it on.

"Wait!" shouted Franklin as he ran to Constable Raccoon.

"Well now," said the constable. "Whose helmet is that?"

"It's mine," Franklin replied, looking at Fox and Beaver. "And I like it!"

"I like it, too," said Constable Raccoon. "It fits you properly, and you'll be seen from a mile away. Be safe! Be seen!"

Franklin took a deep breath. "Is it too late for me to try out for my safety sticker?"

Constable Raccoon smiled. "You're just in time," he answered.

Franklin finished the course perfectly and received his own shiny safety sticker. Then he rode home as fast as he could.

"I knew all my hand signals!" Franklin told his parents. "Look at the sticker I earned."

"Congratulations," said his mother.

"I knew you could do it," said his father. "Did everyone like your new helmet?"

Franklin grinned. "I don't know," he replied.
"But I sure do!"

Activities

Word Search

Franklin always wears a helmet when he rides his bike. In the puzzle below, circle words from the story. You'll find the words going up, down, across and diagonally.

```
M H A N D L E B A R
B O S E C O T G D I
A Y T F H E M W G R
K T H O V C J H B L
E E I L R I D E I O
L F Q Z U C B E C W
K A R A L L Y L Y U
C S P Q E S A C C T
U V F W S Y U Z L P
B H E L M E T N E E
```

BICYCLE   RALLY

BUCKLE   RIDE

HANDLEBAR   RULES

HELMET   SAFETY

MOTORCYCLE   WHEEL

Search and Find

Constable Raccoon wears a hat with a badge on the front. How many badges can you find in this picture? Circle each one.

I found __11__ badges.

Word Scramble

Fill in the blanks by unscrambling the letters in each box.

1. Franklin's new helmet is white and S̶i̶LVer.

   | l e s r i v |

2. Before the Bike Safety Rally, Franklin practises his
   hand _____. | s l a s i n g |

3. When Franklin gets to the rally, he leaves his bicycle
   behind the BUSHes. | s h u b e s |

4. Rabbit uses cardboard to make his bike sound like a
   MoTorCYCLe. | t c m o l e c r y o |

5. Everyone who finishes the course without any mistakes gets
   a safety STiCKer. | c r e t i k s |

6. Rabbit thinks that Franklin's new helmet is
   AmaZinG. | g i z n a m a |

Spot the Difference

Circle the picture in each row that is different from the others.

1.

2.

3.

1.

2.

3.

1.

2.

3.

Franklin Forgets

FRANKLIN fed his goldfish every day and tidied his room once a week. He helped his parents rake leaves in the fall and shovel snow in the winter. Franklin liked doing chores. It made him feel very grown-up.

One day, Franklin and his friends were putting the finishing touches on their go-cart. Mr. Mole stopped to admire their work.

"All you need is a horn," he said. "Maybe I'll discover the perfect one on my travels."

"Are you going away?" asked Franklin.

"Just for four days," answered Mr. Mole. "First I have to find someone to do a few chores for me while I'm gone."

"I could do your chores, Mr. Mole," Franklin offered eagerly.

"Thank you, Franklin," replied Mr. Mole. "But it's a big responsibility. I think I need someone a little more grown-up."

"But I'm more grown-up than I used to be," insisted Franklin. "And I do lots of chores at home."

Mr. Mole looked at Franklin thoughtfully.

"All right," he agreed. "You've got the job."

Franklin smiled proudly.

29

That afternoon, Franklin went to Mr. Mole's house to get his instructions. He had three things to remember — collect the mail, fill the birdbath and water the garden.

"And that's *every* day," Mr. Mole reminded him.

Franklin nodded. "I won't forget," he replied.

Early the next morning, Franklin collected Mr. Mole's mail and filled the birdbath. He was about to water the garden when Bear and Beaver came along.

"Do you want to fly kites with us?" asked Bear.

"I can't," answered Franklin. "I have to water these flowers."

"Can't you do it later?" asked Beaver.

Franklin thought for a minute.

"Okay," he said finally. "I'll do it this afternoon."

Franklin ran home for his kite.

It wasn't until suppertime that Franklin remembered the garden.

"I'll water it first thing tomorrow," he decided.

But the next morning, Franklin noticed that the sky was dark and cloudy.

"Hmmm," thought Franklin. "It looks like the rain will water Mr. Mole's flowers for me."

Franklin was wrong. The sky cleared up, the sun shone bright and hot ... and Franklin spent the day swimming. He didn't remember his chores until bedtime.

"I won't forget tomorrow," Franklin declared.

But in the morning, Franklin was too excited
about his baseball game to think of anything else.
After winning, he and Beaver were so busy celebrating
that Franklin forgot again. Then he saw his mother
mailing a letter.

"Oh no!" cried Franklin. "My chores!"
Franklin and Beaver rushed to Mr. Mole's.

34

Franklin's heart sank when he saw Mr. Mole's yard. The birdbath was empty, and the mailbox was full. The flowers lay wilted on the hard, dry earth.

Franklin collected the mail and filled the birdbath, but he didn't know what to do about the flowers.

"Maybe they'll perk up if you give them lots of water," suggested Beaver.

"Good idea!" said Franklin. "I'll let the hose run all night."

The next morning, Franklin and Beaver discovered that things had gone from bad to worse. The garden was flooded, and the flowers were ruined.

Franklin hurried to turn off the hose.

"What are you going to do?" asked Beaver.

Franklin thought hard.

"Maybe I could plant the paper flowers I made at camp," he said. "They might look real."

Franklin raced home to get his flowers. He and Beaver planted them, row upon row, in the soggy ground.

"How does it look?" asked Franklin.

"Like a bunch of paper flowers stuck in a mud pie," answered Beaver.

Franklin felt like crying. The garden looked terrible, and Mr. Mole was coming home that afternoon.

Franklin couldn't stop thinking about the garden all morning. After lunch, he waited anxiously by Mr. Mole's gate.

At last, Franklin saw Mr. Mole coming down the road.

Franklin's tummy flip-flopped.

"Hello, Franklin," said Mr. Mole. He reached into his bag and pulled out a shiny new horn.

"I didn't forget," he said cheerfully.

"But I did," Franklin said in a shaky voice. "I forgot to water your garden. Now it's ruined. I ... I'm sorry."

"Now, now, Franklin," said Mr. Mole. "I'm sure things can't be *that* bad."

Then he opened his gate and gasped.

38

"It's all my fault, Mr. Mole," Franklin said sadly. "You were right. I'm not grown-up enough."

"Well, the garden *is* a bit of a mess," said Mr. Mole. "But it took a lot of courage to tell me the truth. Taking responsibility for a mistake is a very grown-up thing to do."

"If I help you plant new flowers, would that be grown-up, too?" Franklin asked hopefully.

Mr. Mole smiled. "It sure would," he said.

39

Before long, Mr. Mole's garden was growing again.

"You know, Franklin," said Mr. Mole, "with all your help, my garden looks better than ever."

"Well," Franklin replied, "I *do* have two green thumbs!"

Activities

What's Wrong with This Picture?

On a hot summer day, Franklin and his friends have lots of fun playing with their go-cart. But there are many things in this picture that **are** usually seen only in winter. Can you find them? Circle each one.

Connect the Dots

Franklin and his friends need a horn for their go-cart.
Connect the dots to see who gives them a shiny new horn.

Colouring Fun

Franklin Helps Out

48

FRANKLIN could count by twos and tie his shoes. He liked to help Mr. Owl in the classroom, and he always lent a hand to friends and neighbours. But one day, Franklin was a little *too* helpful.

Franklin's class was going on a nature hike. Mr. Owl asked everyone to bring back something for the school nature display.

He reminded the students to leave living things in the woods, where they belonged.

Then he pointed out where Franklin and his friends might find some interesting nature objects.

Franklin could hardly wait to collect something special.

"Let's go this way," he said to Snail.

But Snail didn't hear because he was too busy looking at fungus.

Then, without asking, Franklin scooped up Snail.

"I'll give you a ride," said Franklin.

Snail was startled. He hadn't finished exploring yet.

Minutes later, Franklin spotted some milkweed. He put Snail down and blew on the pods. The seeds floated in the breeze.

"That looks like fun," thought Snail. He found a whole pod of seeds for himself, but when he huffed and puffed, nothing budged.

So Snail searched until he found a pod with one small seed. He was about to blow on it when Franklin picked him up.

"We're on our way," said Franklin. "I'll give you a hand, Snail."

Snail sighed. He had wanted to blow on a seed, too.

There were lots of wonderful things to collect in the woods.

Beaver stuffed her backpack with pine cones, leaves and rocks.

"How many things do you have?" she asked Snail.

"None so far," answered Snail. "I'm waiting to find something really special."

After lunch, Bear discovered a wasps' nest.

"Wasps sting if you bother them," warned Beaver.

But Bear insisted the nest was empty.

Franklin set Snail near a log and took a closer look. Then he heard a buzzing sound. "Oh no," he cried.

A cloud of angry wasps flew out.

"Run!" shouted Fox.

Franklin and his friends ran screaming down the path.

"That was close," panted Beaver.
"That's the fastest I've ever run," said Goose.
"Me, too," said Franklin. "How about you, Snail?"
But Snail wasn't there to answer.

Franklin suddenly remembered that he'd left Snail behind.

"Maybe the wasps stung Snail!" cried Franklin. "I should have taken him with me."

Franklin and his friends raced back to the nest. There was no sign of the wasps and no sign of Snail.

"Snail?" called Franklin. "Snail? Where are you?"

Snail had no idea that his friends were worried about him. He was busy exploring a network of termite tunnels.

Snail was puzzled when he heard Franklin's frantic calls.

"Here I am," said Snail, as he crawled out of the log. Franklin rushed toward him. "Are you all right?"

"Of course," giggled Snail.

Everyone was relieved to see that Snail was safe.

Snail didn't understand all the fuss. "I'm fine," he said. "But I need to collect something."

"I'll help you," said Franklin, stooping to pick up his little friend.

"I can do it myself," said Snail.

But Franklin insisted.

Snail's head drooped and he let out a big sigh.

57

Franklin made sure he helped Snail all afternoon.

When Franklin found seeds, he put them into Snail's bag.

When he found beautiful pebbles, he kept one for himself and gave the other to Snail.

He even picked a leaf for Snail, although Snail could have done it by himself.

Franklin collected so many things that Snail could barely move.

When it was almost time to go back to school, Snail still hadn't collected anything that *he* wanted.

Franklin offered to find something else.

Snail was annoyed. "I want to find my own special things," he said firmly. Then he set off alone.

Franklin was hurt and puzzled.

"I just wanted to help," he told his friends. "Snail is small, and he doesn't move very fast."

"But he's good at doing things for himself," said Beaver. "In his own way."

Rabbit pointed to the cliff. Snail was climbing straight up the side.

"I told you," said Beaver.

"Wow," said Franklin. "It looks like Snail doesn't always need my help."

Soon, Snail slid down the cliff and showed his friends a sparkling quartz crystal.

Everyone oohed and aahed.

"That's the best find yet," said Franklin.

Snail smiled proudly.

Just then, Mr. Owl's whistle blew. "Better hurry back," said Beaver.

Franklin started to pick up Snail, but then he stopped.

"Can I give you a ride, Snail?" he asked.

"Sure," said Snail cheerfully. "I like getting help when I really need it."

Franklin ran so fast that some pebbles and leaves fell out of his bag.

"Don't worry," said Snail. "You can have one of my crystals."

"Thanks!" said Franklin.

Snail smiled. "I'm glad I could help."

Activities

Search and Find

Some ladybugs sneaked into Franklin's book bag and now they're all over the classroom! How many ladybugs can you find? Circle each one.

I found 14 ladybugs.

Word Search

Franklin and his friends find lots of interesting things on their nature hike. In the puzzle below, circle words from the story. You'll find the words going up, down, across and diagonally.

T	B	A	D	J	Y	E	Y	K	O
F	U	N	G	U	S	C	A	H	V
W	D	N	M	L	S	I	L	E	D
Q	U	P	N	P	O	H	P	L	E
C	O	L	L	E	C	T	S	P	E
L	P	U	N	S	L	J	I	F	W
I	W	E	G	T	E	S	D	U	K
F	V	Z	I	W	R	E	N	L	L
F	Q	U	A	R	T	Z	D	H	I
B	A	C	K	P	A	C	K	S	M

BACKPACK   HELPFUL

CLIFF   MILKWEED

COLLECT   QUARTZ

DISPLAY   SEEDS

FUNGUS   TUNNELS

Nature Maze

Help Franklin find his way back to Snail.

START

FINISH

Franklin and the Hero

FRANKLIN could count by twos and tie his shoes. He could say the alphabet without stopping, and he was learning how to read. His favourite books were about Dynaroo, the kangaroo superhero. Franklin wanted to be just like Dynaroo.

One day, Franklin and Snail were reading *Dynaroo to the Rescue*.

"Look, Snail," cried Franklin. "Dynaroo pulls Koala out of the quicksand with one mighty tug!"

"Dynaroo's the best," Snail sighed happily.

Franklin agreed. "I want to be as strong as she is."

"I want to be as fast," said Snail.

Franklin had an idea.

"Let's play superheroes," he suggested. "I'm Turtle-roo, strong enough to lift a truck!"

"And I'm Dyna-snail," announced Snail, "faster than a speeding train!"

"Together we'll keep the world safe," declared Franklin.

"Just like Dynaroo," added Snail.

Turtle-roo and Dyna-snail ran outside. They saved their snow fort from a terrible snow monster over and over again.

72

Hours later, Franklin's mother called to them. "Turtle-roo! Dyna-snail! Come inside. I have a big surprise."

When the superheroes were warm and dry, Franklin's mother told them the good news.

"Dynaroo will be autographing her new book at Mr. Heron's bookstore tomorrow morning," she said. "Do you know anyone who would like to go?"

Franklin and Snail jumped up and down and gave each other the Dynaroo salute.

For the rest of the afternoon, Franklin and Snail talked about Dynaroo. They reread all of Dynaroo's adventures and made their plans for the next day. They were both so excited they could hardly eat their dinner or fall asleep that night.

Early in the morning, Franklin and Snail set off for the bookstore. As they rounded a bend in the path, they saw Mrs. Muskrat searching through the snow.

"I dropped my house key," she explained. "And now I'm locked out. Can you help me find it?"

Franklin looked at Snail.

"But ..." Snail began.

"Come on, Snail," Franklin decided. "This shouldn't take two superheroes long at all."

Franklin was wrong. They dug and dug without finding the key.

"We may not find it until the snow melts," Mrs. Muskrat said finally. "It's time to call off the search."

Franklin and Snail breathed sighs of relief and turned to go.

"If you could pile some snow under the window," continued Mrs. Muskrat, "maybe we could get in that way."

"But, Mrs. Muskrat," Franklin said, then stopped. Mrs. Muskrat was shivering.

So Franklin huffed and puffed and rolled a huge snowball to the kitchen window. He climbed on top and pushed and shoved until the window opened just enough for Snail to crawl through.

Up and over the ledge went Snail, across the counter, down the wall, over the floor and up the door. Finally, Snail turned the door handle.

"Hurray!" shouted Franklin.

"This calls for hot chocolate and cake!" declared Mrs. Muskrat.

Franklin and Snail looked at the kitchen clock.

"Thank you, Mrs. Muskrat," said Franklin. "But ... you see ..." And he finally told her all about Dynaroo.

"Well, off you go!" exclaimed Mrs. Muskrat. "I can thank both of you properly another time."

Franklin and Snail hurried to town and rushed into the bookstore.

But no one was there. They had missed Dynaroo.

Franklin's shoulders slumped, and Snail started to cry. As they turned to go, Mr. Heron came out of the back room.

"We've been waiting for you," he said with a smile.

Mr. Heron stepped aside, and there was Dynaroo.

Franklin and Snail gasped in amazement.

"I couldn't leave until I'd met two real-life heroes," Dynaroo announced.

Franklin and Snail were confused.

"Mrs. Muskrat phoned and told us what happened," explained Mr. Heron. "You are both heroes to her."

"But we were just pretending to be heroes," said Franklin. "Real heroes are super fast and super strong."

"Sometimes they are," agreed Dynaroo. "But there are other ways to be a hero."

Franklin thought for a moment. Then he smiled.

"I never knew that helping someone could make you a hero," he said.

Dynaroo gave both Franklin and Snail a copy of her new book, *Dynaroo's Jungle Adventure*. Inside each was a dedication from Dynaroo.

Franklin read his aloud. "To Franklin, my heroic friend."

Franklin and Snail gave Dynaroo a big hug, and Mr. Heron took everyone's picture.

Later that night, when Snail's family had left and Mrs. Muskrat's cake was all gone, Franklin went to bed with his new book and a flashlight. He planned to read the whole story. But soon he was sound asleep.

Even superheroes need their rest.

Activities

Connect the Dots

Franklin and Snail love to read together. Do you know who their favourite stories are about? Connect the dots to find out.

Meeting Dynaroo Maze

Help Franklin and Snail get to the bookstore in time to meet Dynaroo.

START

FINISH

Colouring Fun

Spot the Difference

Circle the picture in each row that is different from the others.

1.

2.

3.

1.

2.

3.

1.

2.

3.

Answers

Word Search – p. 22

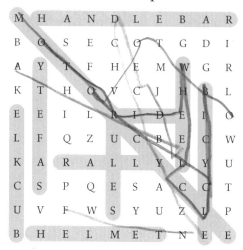

Search and Find – p. 23

There are 14 badges.

Word Scramble – p. 24

1. silver
2. signals
3. bushes
4. motorcycle
5. sticker
6. amazing

Spot the Difference – p. 25

Franklin – #3
bicycle – #1
Constable Raccoon – #2

What's Wrong with This Picture – pp. 42–43

snow on bush
toboggan
earmuffs
icicles
ski poles
Christmas tree
Beaver's winter hat
snowshoes
mittens
snow shovel
skates
skis
snowman
scarf

Search and Find – p. 64–65

There are 22 ladybugs.

Word Search – p. 66

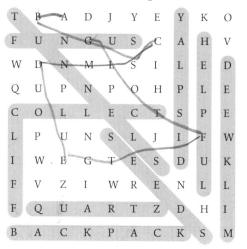

Nature Maze – p. 67

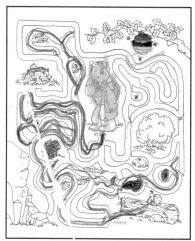

Meeting Dynaroo Maze – p. 85

Spot the Difference – p. 87

Dynaroo – #2
Franklin – #3
Mr. Heron – #2